SESAME STREET

Featuring
Jim Henson's
Sesame Street
Muppets

Puppy Love

by MADELINE SUNSHINE
Illustrated by CAROL NICKLAUS

This educational book was created in cooperation with the Children's
Television Workshop, producers of Sesame Street. Children do not have
to watch the television show to benefit from this book. Workshop
revenues from this product will be used to help support CTW
educational projects.

A SESAME STREET/GOLDEN PRESS BOOK

It was a quiet morning on Sesame Street. Ernie and Bert were just finishing breakfast when the telephone rang.

"Hello?" said Ernie. "Um-hm. Sure. Don't worry, you can count on us. Good-by!"

"Ernie, who was that on the phone?" asked Bert. "Who can count on us?"

"That was Barbara," said Ernie. "She called to ask us a favor, and I said we'd do it."

"Oh, good," said Bert. "What kind of favor?"

"Oh, it's nothing much, Bert," said Ernie. "I just said we'd take care of Barbara's dog, Hulk, while she visits her grandmother today."

"Ernie, we don't know the first thing about taking care of dogs!" shouted Bert.

"Don't worry, Bert. There's nothing to it," said Ernie. "Come on. We have to meet Barbara and Hulk."

"Hi, Bert. Hi, Ernie," said Barbara when they all met in front of Mr. Hooper's store. "I'm glad you can take care of Hulk. I know you'll do a really terrific job. I have to go now or I'll miss my bus. Bye!"

"What are we going to do with this dog, huh, Ernie?" asked Bert.

"I've got an idea, Bert," said Ernie as he saw Barkley the dog trotting toward them. "Hi, Barkley. Bert and I have to take care of this cute little puppy. Maybe you can give us a hand. I mean paw."

Barkley grabbed Hulk's leash and began leading the puppy down the street.

"Come on, Bert!" shouted Ernie. "Barkley's taking Hulk for a walk. I guess he's trying to tell us that puppies need exercise."

At last Ernie and Bert caught up with the dogs
and they all walked to the park.

"Fetch, Hulk! Fetch, Barkley!" shouted Bert,
tossing a stick across the lawn.

"Let's play hide and seek!" called Ernie, and he
jumped behind a tree. "Bet you can't find me!"

After a while, Ernie and Bert and Barkley
and Hulk plopped down under a shady tree.
"Boy, am I tired and hungry," said Bert.
"Yeah, so am I," said Ernie.

"Come on, Bert," said Ernie. "Let's take Barkley and Hulk home and feed them some lunch. I bet they're hungry, too."

"You were right, Ernie," said Bert, as Barkley and Hulk ate their dog food. "The dogs really were hungry and thirsty!"

"What should we do now, Bert?" asked Ernie,
when they had all finished eating.

Before Bert could figure out an answer, Barkley
dashed out the door and ran down Sesame Street.

"Barkley, wait! Where are you going?" called Bert.

By the time Ernie and Bert and Hulk ran outside, Barkley was back and he was dragging a long, green garden hose.

"Hey, Bert," said Ernie. "Are you 'thinking what I'm thinking?"

"I don't know, Ernie," said Bert. "What are you thinking?"

"I'm thinking that water washes things," said Ernie.

"You mean things like puppies?" said Bert.

"That's it, Bert," said Ernie. "I'm thinking old Barkley here is telling us that part of taking care of a puppy is keeping him clean. I think he's telling us to give the puppy a bath!"

Bert got the dog shampoo. Ernie got his Rubber
Duckie. They lathered Hulk with soap suds. Then,
while Bert held the puppy gently, Ernie rinsed the suds
off with cool water from the garden hose.

Ernie and Bert dried Hulk and Barkley with
a big towel.

"Now what?" said Bert. "What do we do now?"

"I don't know," said Ernie. "But I think Barkley
does. See? He's brought us his brush."

"He must want us to brush the puppy," said Bert.
He picked up the brush and began to smooth out the
little dog's fur.

"Oh, wow!" said Ernie. "Look how shiny and soft
Hulk's coat is getting."

"Right, Ernie," said Bert. "Let's brush Barkley next."

When Ernie and Bert had brushed both dogs, they decided to go back inside. Bert set Hulk down in the middle of the living room floor. Hulk yawned a big yawn.

"Hey, Ernie," said Bert. "I just thought of something else we could do."

"What's that?" said Ernie.

"We can make the puppy a bed." Bert answered. "We can use this nifty blanket and make him a nice, soft place to sleep."

"Gee, Bert, a nap's not a bad idea," said Ernie
when the dogs were asleep. "In fact, I wouldn't mind
a little nap myself."

But Ernie didn't rest for very long.

"Bert? Ernie?" called Barbara from outside. "I've
come to pick up Hulk."

"We'll be right down," Bert shouted back.

"Hi, Hulk!" said Barbara. "It looks like you've had a good time. Thanks, Ernie. Thanks, Bert. Thanks, Barkley!"

"Aw, it was nothing," said Bert. "We just took him for a walk and played games with him and fed him lunch."

"And washed him and brushed him and let him take a nap," said Ernie.

"And now we're going to miss him," they both said.

"You know, Ernie," said Bert, "taking care of a pet is a lot of work, but it's also a lot of fun. It sure is going to be lonely around here without a dog to take care of."

"Don't worry about it, Bert," said Ernie. "I have a feeling that we're going to have a dog to take care of very soon!"

Long ago, a goat, a rooster, and a donkey decided to try their luck at farming.

"If we work together, we can grow anything," said Goat.
"What should we plant?" asked Rooster.
"How about clover?" suggested Donkey. "I love to
eat clover."

So the three of them pulled up the weeds, plowed the
ground, and planted the clover seeds.

They watered the field every day. Soon the clover began
to grow.

"Is it ready now?" asked the impatient donkey.
"No, not yet," said Rooster.
"If we wait, it will taste nice and sweet," said Goat.

After a few weeks, the clover had grown bigger.

"Is it ready now?" asked Donkey.
"No, not yet," said Rooster.
"Just a little more time and it will be perfect," agreed Goat.

A few days later, they returned to the field.

"Surely it must be ready now," pleaded Donkey.
"One more day and it will be just right," said Rooster.
"Yes, tomorrow we will have a feast," said Goat.

"Tomorrow?" whined Donkey. "Do we have to wait
till tomorrow?"
"It's just one more night," said Rooster.
"By then the clover will be even sweeter," said Goat.

So they agreed they would go to the field together the
next morning.

Donkey, Rooster, and Goat went home. But Donkey couldn't sleep. He kept on thinking about the sweet-smelling clover. At last he said, "I'm going to the field to have one little taste."

When Donkey got to the field, he took a bite of clover. "Mmmm! So good, so sweet," he thought. "Just one more bite."

Then Donkey said to himself, "Oh, no one will notice if I take one more little taste. . ."

And so it went. Donkey couldn't help himself. Although he kept on saying, "Just one more bite," it wasn't long before he had eaten the whole field of clover.

The next morning, Rooster crowed at the crack of dawn.
He and Goat knocked on Donkey's door.
"Wake up, Donkey! It's time to eat our clover!" they shouted.

But Donkey had a terrible stomachache. From inside he moaned, "I'm not feeling well today. Go ahead and eat your share and save some for me."

When Rooster and Goat got to the clover field, they couldn't believe their eyes.

"Someone has eaten our clover!" cried Rooster.
"I'll bet it was Donkey," yelled Goat.

They marched back to Donkey's house, banged on the door, and rushed inside. There was Donkey, lying in bed with a swollen belly.

"We know you ate the clover," accused Rooster.
"Look how big your belly is," agreed Goat.

"Oh, no," argued Donkey. "It wasn't me. One of you must have eaten the clover."

"We will put this to the test," said Rooster. "Let's go to the Well of Truth."

"We will all jump over the well," said Goat. "Anyone who tells a lie will fall in and stay there for two months and one night."

When they got to the Well of Truth, Rooster went first.

He said, "To prove I did not eat the clover
    The Well of Truth I will jump over.
    If I do lie to one and all—
    Into the well I'll surely fall."

Rooster jumped and easily made it over the well.

Goat was next. He swore the same oath.

"To prove I did not eat the clover
 The Well of Truth I will jump over.
 If I do lie to one and all—
 Into the well I'll surely fall."

Goat also jumped over the well with no problem.

It was Donkey's turn.
He looked nervously at the Well of Truth.
"Go ahead!" challenged Rooster.
"Yes, it's your turn, Donkey," said Goat.

Donkey spoke slowly, "To prove I did not eat the clover
The Well of Truth I will jump over.
If I do lie to one and all—
Into the well I'll surely fall."

When Donkey jumped, he fell right into the Well of Truth.
And there he stayed for two months and one night.